# Princess Katie's Kittens

# Princess Katie's Kittens

Collect all the kittens!

Pixie at the Palace
Bella at the Ball

☆

Coming Soon:

Poppy and the Prince
Suki in the Snow
Tilly and the Tiara
Pebbles and the Puppy

Julie Sykes

# Princess Katie's Kittens

## Pixie at the Palace

PICCADILLY PRESS • LONDON

*For Gladys and Joe*

First published in Great Britain in 2012
by Piccadilly Press Ltd,
5 Castle Road, London NW1 8PR
www.piccadillypress.co.uk

A catalogue record for this book is available
from the British Library

ISBN: 978 1 84812 238 3 (paperback)

3 5 7 9 10 8 6 4 2

Printed and bound by CPI Group (UK) Ltd,
Croydon, CR0 4YY
Cover design by Simon Davis
Cover illustration by Sue Hellard
Inside illustrations by Richard Morgan

# Chapter 1

# A Journey

The silver Rolls-Royce stopped outside Starlight Palace and Princess Katie of Tula unfastened her seatbelt.

'Thank you for picking me up, Mr Bentley.'

'You're welcome, Princess. Homework now, is it?'

'We didn't get any today so I'm free to go riding!'

Princess Katie bubbled with excitement. She loved horses and had her own pony, a dapple-grey mare called Misty. Katie visited Misty every day, even though being a princess meant that she was sometimes too busy to ride her.

Mr Bentley held open the car door as Katie picked up her school bag and climbed out. A fluffy white Persian cat was sitting on the stone steps that led up to the palace.

'Hello, Crystal,' said Katie, stretching out her hand.

Crystal stared back, haughtily twitched her whiskers, then stood up and walked away.

Katie sighed. She'd been trying to stroke Crystal ever since she was a tiny kitten, but the royal cat was very choosy about her friends. The only time she let Katie touch her was if she wanted feeding.

'I wish you were a cuddly cat!' called Katie. 'I'd let you sleep on my bed.'

Crystal kept walking and Katie swallowed her disappointment. Never mind. At least Misty was always pleased to see her, even though the pony was too big to sleep in her bedroom. Giggling at the thought, Katie hurried indoors.

The silver-grey kitten with black stripes peered round the table leg. His brother and sisters were lying together in their basket. Silently, he crept towards them, dodging behind the bin when his tortoiseshell sister turned her head. Had she seen him? He stood very still until she settled down, yawned lazily and closed her orange eyes. Bunching his tiny body, the kitten pounced and landed in the basket on top of every-one. At once, his ginger brother sprang up, hissing in surprise, claws drawn.

'Got you!' the kitten giggled.

'Meow!' The ginger kitten cuffed him playfully.

His sisters – one black and white, one

grey and white, and one tortoiseshell – jumped on his back.

The kitten squeaked with pleasure. He loved a good play fight. Rolling about, he batted at everyone with his paws and tail.

The fun lasted ages until, suddenly, all the kittens ran out of energy. They flopped down in their basket, their tiny bodies squashed together so it was impossible to tell where one kitten ended and the next began.

*We're getting bigger,* thought the silver-grey kitten sleepily. Soon their mother would take them outside and teach them how to hunt. He could hardly wait! Mum told exciting stories of the great outdoors. She was an excellent hunter, which was lucky, as there was never enough to eat at home.

'Our owner, Mrs Baxter, doesn't mean to let us go hungry,' Mum told the kittens. 'She's old and doesn't have much money.'

Mum was out hunting now. Each day she left the kittens alone for a little longer, preparing them for the day when they would be old enough to go out into the world by themselves. A door opened and Mrs Baxter shuffled in, carrying a large box with black marks on the outside. Ears pricked, the kitten sat up. This looked interesting. Mrs Baxter put the box on the floor and gave him a sad smile.

'Hello, little one. Have you just woken up?'

Slowly, she bent down and scratched the kitten behind his pixie-like ears.

That was so good! Purring with delight, he rubbed his head against her knobbly fingers. Something wet splashed on his head.

Ew! He didn't like that!

Indignantly, he shook it away. The wet stuff was leaking from Mrs Baxter's eyes. Was she all right? The kitten had never seen that happen before. Mrs Baxter sniffed, pulled a tissue from her pocket and blew her nose loudly.

'I'm sorry. I wish I didn't have to do this. I can't afford to keep you and I don't know where to go for help. I'll leave you somewhere safe. You'll be away from the road but in a place where lots of people walk. Someone will find you. They'll give you a better home than I can.'

The kitten was baffled. What did she mean? It sounded like she was sending him away. But he wasn't ready to go yet and he hadn't said goodbye to Mum. He meowed in protest as Mrs Baxter lifted him by the

scruff of his neck, supporting his bottom
with her hand, and gently put him into the
box. Sheets of newspaper lined the floor. It
wasn't as cosy as the kitten's basket and it
rustled when he moved, but it was comfortable enough. Then he heard a frightened
squeak. That was his black-and-white sister.
The silver-grey kitten jumped at the sides of
the box, wanting to climb out and comfort
her.

'Easy there. I'm not leaving you on your
own.' Mrs Baxter lowered his four sisters in
beside him, followed by his brother.

'What's going on?' they squealed.

'It's all right. She's not going to hurt us.'
The kitten busied himself licking everyone,
like Mum did, until they'd calmed down.

Suddenly, the box began to wobble. Mrs

Baxter grunted as she struggled to lift it. The kittens pricked their ears in alarm, but the silver-grey kitten remembered what Mrs Baxter had told him.

'She's taking us somewhere nice,' he said confidently.

They travelled in a car. The kitten knew about cars from Mum. She'd told him never to run in front of them and not to fall asleep inside one either, because then you might get lost. Mrs Baxter had put a lid on the box. It was dark, with only a few small holes to let in air. The kitten's green eyes widened as they adjusted to the gloom. He peered through a hole, but it wasn't big enough to see through. He sat up straight, ears pricked as he tried to follow the direction they were taking, but it was a bumpy ride and he soon got confused. Sighing softly, the kitten lay down with his brother and sisters.

A long while later, the drive was over. As Mrs Baxter lifted the box out of the car, the kitten's nose twitched with excitement. What was that delicious smell? It was the same scent that clung to Mum when she'd been out hunting. It tickled his nose and made him want to run and jump. Suddenly, he remembered what it was.

It was the smell of the great outdoors! It was the place Mum called the woods. The kitten purred with excitement. 'We're in a forest.'

He could hardly sit still. He wished Mrs Baxter would hurry up. She was walking slowly and he couldn't wait to get out of the box and explore his new surroundings.

At last, Mrs Baxter stopped and carefully lowered the box to the ground. Pulling back a corner of the lid, she stroked each kitten on the head.

'Good luck,' she whispered.

The kitten rubbed his head against her hand. As she pulled away, he glimpsed a tall tree stretching above him. The lid closed suddenly.

'Wait,' he cried in frustration.

But all he could hear were Mrs Baxter's footsteps fading as she walked away. Angrily, the kitten swiped the side of the box. Was that it? Why had she brought them here if she wasn't going to let them out?

'I'm hungry. When's Mum coming?' asked his brother.

'I'm hungry too,' his sisters echoed.

Mum wouldn't come. How could she? She wouldn't know where to find them. The kitten decided it was up to him to look after everyone. It was an exciting thought, but a scary one too. He stood tall, holding his tail up straight behind him.

'I'm in charge now. Let's get out of here! Then we'll look for something to eat.'

Reaching up, he tried to bat the lid open. He wasn't tall enough. He tried again, stretching right up, leaning his front paws against the side of the box and lifting his head to push it off. Still he couldn't quite reach. Full of frustration, he bunched his tiny body and jumped at the lid. His head batted it with a soft *thunk*. The kitten leapt again and again until suddenly the lid lifted, letting in a breath of fresh air and a rich woody smell. That was so good! Feeling encouraged, he sprang at the lid like a tiny tiger, bracing his body for the bump.

The lid of the box opened suddenly. Light and air flooded in as the kitten hurtled out. There was a surprised yelp, then two soft hands caught him round his middle, sweeping him upwards until he was face to face with a young girl. She had friendly green eyes and long blond hair which swept down her shoulders.

'Look!' she exclaimed, her mouth widening into a smile. 'A kitten!'

# Chapter 2

# Pixie

After changing out of her school uniform, Princess Katie went riding on Misty. Sitting back in the saddle she squeezed the reins, asking Misty to walk. Her eyes shone with happiness as she patted the pony's dapple-grey neck.

'That was brilliant fun. Can we do it again?'

Miss Blaze, the royal riding instructress, laughed.

'Misty needs a rest after all that galloping.

We'll ride this way tomorrow if you like.'

'Yes, please,' said Katie eagerly. 'Tomorrow's Saturday, so we can stay out for longer.'

'What about your extra dance lesson?' asked Miss Blaze.

Katie scowled, then, remembering that wasn't very princess-like, quickly turned it into a smile.

'I'd forgotten about that. I'm learning a new dance to perform at Mum's birthday ball. Maybe if I do well today, Madame Quickstep will let me off her lesson tomorrow.'

Katie fell silent as she ran through the dance moves in her head. There was one really tricky bit, but she was good at dancing, so it shouldn't take long to get the hang of it. Deep in thought, Katie almost didn't notice the large cardboard box in the middle of the path.

'What's that?' she exclaimed, reining Misty in.

From inside the box came a funny squeaking noise and lots of scrabbling. Slipping her feet out of her stirrups, Katie jumped off Misty and handed her reins to Miss Blaze.

'*Please look after us*,' she said, reading the words written across the side of the box.

'Princess, wait! Let me open it,' said Miss Blaze, hurriedly sliding off her horse.

Katie was already lifting the lid. She squealed in surprise as a bundle of fur leapt into her hands.

'Look!' she exclaimed. 'A kitten!'

Holding the kitten up to her face, Katie

examined him. He was a pretty silver-grey tabby with black stripes, green eyes and pointed ears that were a little too large for his tiny body.

'Your ears make you look like a pixie,' she giggled.

The kitten stared at her solemnly. The squeaking in the box was getting louder and he tried to wriggle free.

'What's that?'

Tucking the kitten under one arm, Katie looked inside the box.

'More kittens! Oh, you poor things! Doesn't your owner want you any more? I'll have you! I'll have to ask my Mum and Dad first, but I bet they'll say yes, especially when they see how cute you are.'

Bending down, Princess Katie put the tabby back in the box so that she could stroke all of the kittens. They had silky-soft fur and long whiskers that tickled her hand, making her giggle. They were all eager for her attention, but the tabby was the boldest, mewing loudly and butting her with his head when she stopped stroking him.

'Princess Katie.'

Katie looked up in surprise. Miss Blaze sounded worried.

'We have to go home.'

'Good,' said Katie. 'I think the kittens are hungry. How are we going to get them back? If I lead the horses, could you carry the box?'

Miss Blaze shook her head.

'The box is too big to carry that far.

Besides, we'll be late if we walk. Leave the kittens here and I'll come back for them in my car.'

Katie's stomach tightened in panic. 'We can't! They might escape. And what if someone else comes along? I found them first. I want them!'

'It won't be for long,' said Miss Blaze gently. 'We'll put the lid back on the box so the kittens can't escape, and hide it safely in the bushes.'

'I'll wait here then,' said Katie, scared that something bad might happen if they left the kittens on their own. 'Could you take Misty home for me?'

Miss Blaze shook her head. 'You know I can't do that. I'd be in very big trouble if I left you here alone.'

'But . . .' said Katie.
She swallowed hard
to stop the tears
brimming in her
eyes.

'It won't be for
long. The kittens will
be fine,' said Miss
Blaze firmly.

Reluctantly, Katie patted each cat goodbye, leaving the little tabby until last.

'Be good, Pixie,' she whispered. 'I'll be
back for you soon, I promise.'

Wishing she didn't have to shut the kittens
up again, Katie replaced the lid of the box.

'Where shall we hide them?'

'Over here,' said Miss Blaze, pointing to a
large bush with huge red flowers.

Katie went over and, sinking to her knees, pushed aside the branches so that Miss Blaze could slide the box underneath the bush. She rearranged the leaves so that any passers-by wouldn't notice it hidden there. Twigs snagged on her pink-and-lilac riding hat and her white jodhpurs got covered in dirt. Katie brushed as much of it off as she could before mounting Misty.

'Let's go,' she said, squeezing the pony into a fast trot.

The ride home seemed to take forever. Miss Blaze wouldn't let Katie canter because the ponies had worked hard and needed to cool down. Katie's heart leapt for joy when she glimpsed the huge silver turrets of Starlight Palace rising above the trees. She had lived in the palace all her life and always loved coming home, but she was especially pleased to see it right now.

She rode out of the woods, skirting the wide green lawns of the formal garden and taking the path that led to the stables. One of the peacocks was showing off, strutting  along with his jewel-blue feathers outstretched. He looked amazing, but Katie was too worried about the kittens to pay him much atten- tion. The moment she reached the stable yard, she jumped off Misty, ran her stirrups up their leathers and unbuckled the saddle.

'Hi, Katie. What's the hurry?'

Katie looked up and saw her best friend, Becky Philips.

Katie and Becky were both nine years old
and had known each other since they were
babies. They saw each other almost every
day. Becky's mum was the palace house-
keeper and her family lived in their own
special rooms in the west tower.

'Hi, Becky. Guess what? I found a box of
kittens abandoned in the woods! Miss Blaze
is driving me back to get them. Do you
want to come with us?'

'Kittens!' exclaimed Becky, pushing her

curly brown hair out of her eyes. 'Really! What are they like?'

'They're so sweet. The box was too heavy to carry home, so we've hidden it. I just hope the kittens don't escape before we get back.'

Katie's voice shook with worry and Becky squeezed her arm.

'Better hurry then. You put Misty's tack away while I brush her down. I'll go and get her head collar and a dandy brush.'

'Thanks, Becky,' said Katie gratefully as her friend dashed away.

The girls made
Misty comfortable
then turned her out in
the paddock.

Katie checked her
watch. 'My dancing
lesson is in forty minutes. That gives us
plenty of time. We'd better go up to the
palace and tell our mums where we're
going.'

They ran through the gardens, ignoring
the parakeets, who
squawked angrily as
they hared past, and
scattering the red
squirrels perched on
the entrance to the
maze. At the lake,

they paused for a moment to catch their breath before crossing the rose garden and running up the three flights of stone steps next to the tiered lawns at the back of the palace.

Suddenly, the patio door to the family lounge swung open and the queen stepped into the garden. When Katie was in earshot, she called out, 'Hello, darling, you're back at last! The dressmaker's here. She needs you to try your dress on again.

She's waiting for you in the sewing room.'

Katie's face fell. 'I can't,' she panted. 'I'm going back to the woods with Becky and Miss Blaze to rescue some stray kittens we found.'

'Stray kittens!' exclaimed the queen, her face wrinkling with surprise. 'But you've already got a cat.'

'Crystal's not mine, she's the royal cat,' said Katie. 'Please, Mum! I have to rescue these kittens. They're too little to be left alone.'

'I'm sorry, Katie, but my birthday ball is in two weeks. You have to go for a fitting or your dress won't be ready in time. Run along now, sweetie, and we'll talk about the kittens later.'

'But I've got my dancing lesson later,' said Katie, clenching her hands together.

'Come and see me after dancing then,' said

the queen, going back inside and closing the door.

Katie's stomach tightened with fear. She couldn't disobey her mum but she had to save the kittens. Turning to Becky, she wailed, 'What am I going to do now?'

# Chapter 3

# Missing

The little tabby kitten loved the girl with the soft hands. Her name was Princess Katie and she'd called him 'Pixie'. She was very good at stroking. She didn't press too hard and she brushed his fur in the right direction so that it lay flat. She knew exactly where to rub him when he butted her hand for more. Pixie sensed that Princess Katie liked animals. She had two with her, huge creatures with long legs and a warm, sweet smell. The animals seemed to trust Princess Katie, and Pixie trusted her too. When she placed him back in the box and shut the lid, Pixie thought she was taking him home.

'What's happening?' his tortoiseshell sister squeaked in alarm.

'Shhh,' Pixie mewed confidently. 'We're safe now.'

But Princess Katie didn't take the kittens home. Instead, she left the box in a dark place. Pixie pressed his face against the side and peered through an air hole but not even a glimmer of light shone through it. Pixie could hardly believe it. What was going on? Why had Princess Katie left them? Anxiously, he paced round the box until his brother and sisters complained that he was treading on them.

Pixie's stomach growled hungrily. If Princess Katie wasn't going to take the kittens home, then he'd better find food for everyone. Pleased to have something to do, he stood up.

'I'm going to get us something to eat,' he said.

Pixie jumped at the lid of the box, but, no matter how hard he batted it, he couldn't get it to stay open. Something seemed to be forcing it back. But he didn't give up. He kept going until, finally, after lots of jumping, the lid stayed open a little. Now Pixie could see that a branch was stopping it from opening properly. Crouching on the floor, Pixie sized up the gap. If he made himself very small, he might be able to squeeze through it. Using his brother as a stepping stone, he reached up and hooked his claws over the side of the box. He hung on tightly and pulled himself up.

Pixie's bottom and tail swung wildly and his hind paws scrabbled against the box's side. He forced his head through the gap, panting, and he stayed there for a moment, catching his breath. Then, as he pulled up his back paws, he overbalanced and toppled forwards. He reached out to save himself but he couldn't get a grip. Branches snagged at his fur, slowing him down until he landed in a pile of leaves with a soft *thud*.

Pixie's bones ached but, remembering

what his mother had taught him, he sprang up and stared around, checking for danger. To his relief, there was none. Cautiously, Pixie forced his way through the bush until he broke out into the open. Ears pricked and whiskers twitching, he stood on the forest path and sniffed the air. There were so many new and wonderful smells. Pixie felt much braver now. Paws tingling with excitement, he set out to explore.

'Princess Katie, if you stopped watching the clock and watched where you were going, you might learn this dance more quickly!' said Madame Quickstep, the royal dance teacher.

Princess Katie blushed. 'Sorry, Madame.'

'Let's start from the beginning. Go back to the middle of the room.' Pushing her glasses back on her nose, Madame Quickstep signalled for the pianist to start playing.

Katie stood very still, listening to the opening bars of the music on the piano and counting herself in. *One, two, three and start.* Gracefully, she stepped forward, lifting her arms out to the side and swinging her hips. *Step, two, three, turn, jump, jump, point. Shimmy across the room and jump again.* A picture of a tiny kitten with pointed ears floated into her mind. Unwillingly, Katie pushed it away. She mustn't think about Pixie. If she didn't get this dance right, Madame Quickstep would never let her out of the lesson.

Katie concentrated on her moves, her gold dance shoes tapping out a beat in time with the music. She'd almost finished. Now for the tricky bit, *run, leap and fly.* Landing gracefully, Katie did a perfect pirouette and came to a stop with her hands high in the air.

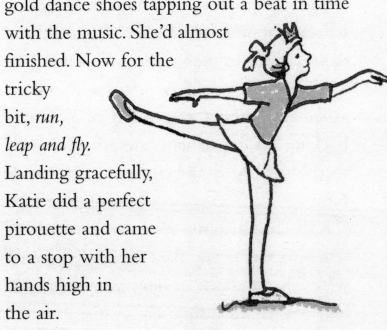

'Bravo!' said Madame Quickstep, clapping loudly. 'I knew you could do it! We'll finish there and I'll see you tomorrow.'

'Thank you.' Katie curtsied to Madame Quickstep and the pianist, then hurried out of the room.

She ran down the corridor to the spiral staircase at the end. Katie's room was on the top floor of the south tower. There was a lift, but Katie preferred to use the stairs, especially when she was in a hurry. Kicking off her dance shoes, she raced up to the top floor and burst into her bed-room.

Katie had a round room with two huge windows that overlooked the lake. The walls were lilac and the ceiling was midnight-blue, dotted with tiny stars that sparkled in the dark. She had an enormous four-poster bed, hung with lilac and silver drapes, and a matching duvet and curtains.

Running into the large dressing room, Katie threw her shoes on the floor, unzipped her dress and removed her tiara. Katie loved dressing up, but today she wished that Madame Quickstep had let her dance in her jodhpurs. It would have been so much quicker. There was no time to put anything away, so Katie left her clothes in a heap and hoped Mum wouldn't suddenly decide to inspect her room. Princesses were supposed to be tidy!

Katie's heart was pounding as she ran back downstairs. Would Becky and Miss Blaze be back yet? Did they have the kittens with them? What would they feed them? Not the same cat food that Crystal ate, that would be too rich for the kittens. By the time she reached the stables, Katie was gasping for breath. There was no one about, but Miss Blaze's green car was in the parking area.

'Becky,' called Katie, 'where are you?'

'Here!' Becky poked her head out of the

hay barn and waved Katie over. 'We've got them! Miss Blaze is just checking them over.' Katie darted into the barn. Miss Blaze was sitting by a cardboard box with the ginger kitten in her hand.

'This one's a boy,' she said, checking under his tail. 'He's a bit thin, but his eyes are bright, his nose is clean and he hasn't got any fleas.'

She held the kitten out to Katie. 'There

you go. Five healthy kittens. Four girls and a boy.'

'Five?' Katie took the kitten with both hands, supporting it carefully as she leaned over the box. Her heart sank like a stone. 'There's one missing!'

'I don't think so,' said Miss Blaze. 'There

were only five kittens in the box when we collected it.'

An icy feeling swept over Katie. There had definitely been six kittens when she first found them. The ginger one she was holding, the little tortoiseshell, the pure white one, the cute grey and white one, the black one with the white tummy and paws – and Pixie, the silver-grey kitten with the black tiger stripes.

So where was Pixie now?

Katie began to tremble. 'We've got to go back to the woods,' she said. 'Pixie's missing!'

## Chapter 4

# Mouse Hunt!

The great outdoors was even more exciting than Pixie had imagined. There were so many different sounds and smells! Pixie's ears and whiskers twitched non-stop as he took them all in.

A small creature fluttered past. It flew a

loop, then landed on a clump of flowers. Pixie quivered with excitement. What was that? On silent paws, he crept closer. The thing had pretty blue wings that kept opening and shutting. It wouldn't make much of a snack, but it looked fun to play with. When the creature suddenly took off, Pixie went after it. He scampered along, leaping in the air as it spiralled out of reach.

'Whiskers!' he
squeaked, when
finally it disappeared.

Pixie wandered on,
enjoying his new free-
dom. The smells were so much nicer than
anything he'd ever experienced before. As a
particularly delicious smell wafted towards
him, Pixie stopped, thrust his nose under the
bush it was coming from and took a deep
breath.

'Mmmmm!'

His mouth watered. Crawling under the
bush, he followed the scent right to the
middle and there he found a tiny animal
perched on a branch. Its beady eyes were
bright with fear, its long whiskers trembling.

'Mouse!'

Mum used to bring mice home for the kittens sometimes. Unsheathing his claws, Pixie wriggled his bottom and sprang. There was a frightened squeak and a rush of air. The mouse vanished into the undergrowth, and Pixie crashed into the branch it had been sitting on and dropped to the floor. Leaping up, he gave chase until finally the mouse scurried up a tree. Experimentally, Pixie tapped the tree's trunk with a paw. Should he go after the mouse? It was a long way up. What if he got stuck or fell and hurt himself? Who would look after his brother and sisters then? Reluctantly, Pixie let the mouse go.

The chase had made him very hungry. Knowing there were mice in the woods made Pixie determined to catch one for tea. He walked until his legs ached and his paw pads were sore. Plonking himself down on his bottom, Pixie gave himself a quick wash. That felt better. But if only he wasn't so ravenously hungry!

Looking around the unfamiliar space,

Pixie realised the light was fading. It was time to go back. If he was lucky, he'd catch a mouse on his way. Pixie stood up and stretched his legs. But which way *was* back? In the failing light, the forest looked the same in every direction. Pixie hesitated, unsure which way to go.

Princess Katie gently lowered the ginger kitten into the box.

'Please, Miss Blaze! We can't leave Pixie alone in the woods. He's too little.'

Miss Blaze ran a hand through her short dark hair. 'Now you mention it, I do remember the  tabby. He was the one that jumped out of the box when you first opened it.'

'Yes! That's the one,' cried Katie, excitedly.

'He must have somehow climbed out.' Miss Blaze sounded concerned. 'We'd better go and look for him. You two, go and wait in my car while I lock up the barn. We don't want the other kittens wandering off while we're gone.'

Katie threw herself at Miss Blaze and hugged her tightly. Then, remembering her manners, she quickly added, 'Thank you, Miss Blaze.'

Katie and Becky raced to the car and, by the time the riding instructress got into the driving seat, they were sitting impatiently in the back.

It didn't take long to drive to the woods. Katie and Becky jumped out of the car and ran on ahead. They had no trouble recognising the bush where the kittens had been left. The ground was covered with footprints and hoof marks. Sinking to her knees, Princess Katie pushed back the branches.

'Pixie!' she called loudly. 'Pixie, here, kitty! We've come to take you home.'

Katie waited, her head tilted, as she listened for an answering cry or the patter of tiny paws. The silence stretched out around her.

'Pixie!' she called again.

'Did you find him?' Miss Blaze arrived as Katie and Becky were wriggling backwards out of the bush.

Katie's heart was hammering and her voice trembled as she answered. 'He's not here.'

'He can't have gone far,' said Miss Blaze briskly. 'Becky, you search over here, Princess Katie you search there and I'll take that bit.'

Everyone spread out. When they didn't find Pixie, Miss Blaze widened the search again. Katie's eyes were everywhere, from the dusty ground to the top of the trees. What if Pixie had climbed a tree and got stuck? If he had, Katie knew she would have

to go after him, no matter how un-princess-like climbing trees was! Scratchy branches snagged at her clothes and hair, but Katie hardly noticed. All that mattered was finding Pixie.

'Princess,' Miss Blaze came up behind Katie making her jump. 'It's time to go now.'

'But we haven't found Pixie,' said Katie with a worried frown.

'I don't think he's here,' replied Miss Blaze. 'He wouldn't have gone far. He's too little. Someone else must have found him and taken him home.'

'But what if they didn't? Pixie might be lost.' Katie swallowed as she struggled not to cry. 'Please, Miss Blaze, can we stay a bit longer?'

Miss Blaze shook her head. 'It's nearly teatime. You know we'll both be in trouble if you're not back in time. And what about the other kittens? They need to be fed. Pixie's an adventurous cat. I'm sure he'll be fine.'

Katie felt torn. Of course she had to get back and look after the other kittens – but what about Pixie? She couldn't bear to think of him alone in the woods at night.

'It's Saturday tomorrow, so no school,' said Becky suddenly. 'We could come back early. Before breakfast, if you can make it? I bet Dad would bring us if I ask him.'

'Would he?' Hope sparkled in Katie's eyes. 'Yes, please, let's do that.'

Katie took one last look around, then, linking arms with Becky, she walked back to the car.

# Chapter 5

# A New Home

'We need to get some kitten food,' said Katie to Miss Blaze as they drove back to the palace.

'I've already sorted that out,' Miss Blaze replied. 'There were a few tins left over from when Crystal was a kitten and I've ordered in more for tomorrow.'

'What about dishes for the food and water?'

'You can use saucers for now. I expect Becky's mum has a stack of old ones somewhere.'

Becky nodded vigorously. 'She has. She hates throwing things away.'

Katie gazed out of the window and let out a big sigh. Where was Pixie now? She hoped that someone had found him and taken him home, but at the same time she felt terribly sad to think she might never see him again.

Arriving back at Starlight Palace, Becky ran off to ask her Mum for old saucers while Katie went to the kitchens to get the kitten food. She didn't need a tin opener as the cans had special rings to open them. As she reached the barn, she met Becky, teetering under a stack of saucers. Miss Blaze opened the food and Katie and Becky spooned out small portions into five saucers, then poured the kittens some water.

The kittens mewed excitedly. Jumping out of their box, they rubbed their little bodies against Katie's and Becky's legs, making the girls giggle.

'They were starving!' Becky exclaimed as the ginger kitten pushed his empty saucer across the floor. 'Shall we give them some more?'

'That's enough for now,' said Miss Blaze. 'If you give them too much to eat in one go, they might get a tummy ache.'

'We'll have to get a comb to groom them,' said Katie as they watched the kittens lick themselves clean.

Miss Blaze helped Katie and Becky carry the saucers to the stables and wash them up in the tack room. Katie rinsed out the sink then checked her watch.

'There's just enough time to move the kittens up to the palace,' she said.

'Where are you going to keep them?' asked Becky.

'In my bedroom.'

Katie was so excited about having her own kittens that she couldn't bear to be parted with them.

'You can come and see them whenever you like,' she added, knowing that Becky couldn't have a cat because they made her dad sneeze.

Miss Blaze offered to help the girls carry the box up to the palace.

'We'll use the lift to go upstairs,' puffed Katie as they entered the south tower.

But as they waited for the lift to arrive, the king appeared.

Miss Blaze and Becky curtsied. 'Hello, your majesty.'

'Hello, ladies. What's in the box — or is it a surprise?' asked the king.

'Kittens!' said Katie, proudly. She explained how they'd rescued them from the woods and how Pixie was still lost. Then she remembered that she hadn't been given permission to keep the kittens yet, and quickly added, 'I can have them, can't I, Dad?'

Thoughtfully, the king rubbed his chin. 'Kittens grow up. And we've already got a cat.'

'Crystal's the royal cat, not mine!' said Katie quickly.

'She's not very cuddly or friendly. Please, Dad, I promise I'll look after them and they'll be no trouble.'

The king laughed. 'I very much doubt that! Kittens are always trouble. They'll be into everything and they'll probably scratch the furniture. Remember what Crystal did to my throne when she was little? It was lucky the furniture maker was able to repair the damage.'

'I'll make sure my kittens behave and I'll get them a scratching post. Please, Dad, please let me keep them,' Katie wheedled.

The king pretended to sigh, then he ruffled his daughter's hair and said, 'All right, then. But they're not allowed in the palace. You can keep them in one of the barns.'

'But they're much too little to stay in the

barns,' said Katie. 'And I'll hardly get to see them. If they share my room, I can make sure they're behaving.'

'You can't keep five kittens in your bed-room,' said the king firmly. 'How about you put them in the boot room? It won't matter so much if they make a mess in there.'

Katie really wanted to have the kittens in her room, but at least she was allowed to keep them. Shaking away her disappointment, she smiled and said, 'Thanks, Dad.'

Miss Blaze helped the girls carry the kittens to the boot room and then it was time for her to go. The kittens seemed very happy with their new home. The moment their box touched the ground, they jumped out to explore. The little tortoiseshell climbed inside one of the king's hiking boots and the white kitten squeezed in beside her. The grey and white kitten pounced on a trainer and tugged its laces. The ginger kitten attacked the hedgehog-shaped boot cleaner, batting it with his tiny paws. The black and white kitten joined in, squeaking in surprise when the hedgehog toppled over.

'That's so cute,' giggled Becky.

Katie's eyes shone. 'It's going to be such fun. We'll have to think up names for them too.'

'Bella for the black and white one,' said Becky. 'I don't know why, but it suits her.' 'It's perfect!' Katie agreed. 'Bella it is, then.'

Katie had a hard time dragging herself away from the kittens, but she couldn't be late for tea. Before she left, she made a note and stuck it on the door, warning everyone to keep it closed, to stop the kittens from wandering off.

'Bye, you beautiful kittens,' Katie said, giving each of them a kiss on the top of their head. 'I'll come and see you again later.'

Luckily for Katie, there were no visitors that evening, so tea was a relaxed meal with only two courses, eaten in the family's private dining room. Katie's little brother Alfie was very excited to learn about the kittens and wanted to see them. Katie and Alfie ate as fast as was polite and hardly tasted the delicious food – chicken, chips and sweetcorn followed by an enormous ice cream sundae topped with strawberries and raspberries.

When the serving staff brought in the king and queen's coffee, Princess Katie asked if she and Alfie could be excused.

The king rolled his eyes. 'So a box of kittens is more important than spending time with your parents?'

Katie grinned. She knew he was only joking.

It was fun showing the kittens to Alfie. Even though her six-year-old brother was often a noisy nuisance, Katie got on well with him most of the time. Alfie loved animals and was excellent with the kittens. He held them carefully, without squeezing them, and was very gentle when he stroked them.

'I like Bella, the
black and white one,
best,' said Alfie.
'Which one's your
favourite, Katie?'

Katie looked at the
kittens. Somehow it
didn't seem right to
have a favourite, but,
if she was honest, she
did have an extra soft
spot for Pixie. She
wondered where he

was now. What if he was still in the woods?
Katie's heartbeat quickened and she swiftly
pushed the thought away. But, no matter how
hard she tried to ignore it, a picture of Pixie
alone in the woods haunted her all evening.

Even when she was soaking in her huge round bath, full to the brim with strawberry-scented bubbles, Katie couldn't stop worrying about Pixie.

'It's no good,' she said, sitting up and reaching for the soap. 'I've got to go back to the woods!'

Katie bathed extra speedily. Wrapping a towel round herself, she padded from her en-suite bathroom into her dressing room. She dressed in jeans and a purple hoodie then, putting her towel back in the bathroom, she went to find her parents.

The king and queen were downstairs watching television, drinking large mugs of hot chocolate. They were most surprised that

Katie wasn't in her pyjamas and even more taken aback that she wanted to go out to the woods.

'The kitten might not even be there, sweetheart,' said the king. 'But what if he is?' said Katie, her green eyes bright with tears.

The queen held out her arms to give Katie a hug.

'Mr Parks, the groundsman, patrols at night. How about we ask him to look for your kitten?' she asked.

'That's a brilliant idea,' said Katie, pulling away. 'Can I go with him? I'm too worried to sleep and I don't have school tomorrow.'

The king and queen both laughed.

'Princess Katie, you're impossible!' said the king. 'I tell you what, if you promise to work extra hard at your dance and perform brilliantly at your mum's birthday ball, then just this once I will ask Mr Parks if you can go with him.'

Katie threw herself at her dad. 'Thank you, Dad! Can Becky come too, because I know she won't be able to sleep either?'

'You're totally impossible!' said the king, chuckling.

## Chapter 6

# Alone in the Woods

Pixie had been walking for ages. Darkness was falling and, even though he could still see quite well, he went full circle three times, ending up exactly where he'd started. Refusing to give up, he plodded on until at last he stumbled on a familiar path. This was the track he'd been looking for, the one that led to his brothers and sisters. Pixie was weak with hunger and tiredness, but success made him walk faster. Soon he reached the bush and, purring with delight, he called, 'I'm back!'

But, when he wriggled under the bush, he found it empty. The box had gone! Shocked and dismayed, Pixie stared at the ground. He was definitely at the right place. The earth smelt faintly of kittens. So where *was* everyone? The evening breeze ruffled his fur and he shivered. He didn't want to stay here on his own. He wanted to be snuggled up with his brother and sisters.

Trying not to panic, Pixie scrambled back onto the path where he nosed around for clues. There were lots of prints on the ground. Curiously, he sniffed at them. The almost-round ones smelt of animal but the other prints smelt of people. Pixie's nose twitched with excitement as he examined the smallest human prints. These smelt just like Princess Katie, but some of them were newer than the others. Suddenly, he had a wild thought. What if Princess Katie had come back for the kittens? That had to be it! She must have returned when he was looking for food.

*Food*, grumbled Pixie's stomach. He was hungrier than he'd ever been in his life. He had to find Princess Katie! At first, it was easy to follow her trail. Even when there weren't any footsteps, Pixie could still detect her flower-like scent on the forest path. He trotted on until the path opened out into a huge rectangular clearing. Pixie hesitated. It was harder to pick up Princess Katie's scent here. There were too many other strange smells, including one that made Pixie's paws tremble – the smell of dog. Mum had smelt like that when she'd been chased once.

There were no dogs here now, though, thank goodness. Nose to the ground, Pixie concentrated on Princess Katie's scent, following the trail into the middle of the clearing.

Pixie pawed at the ground in surprise. He walked in a circle. Then, lifting his nose, he sniffed the air.

Mysteriously, Princess Katie's scent had vanished. Pixie was confused. How could that happen? Unless someone had put *her* in a box and carried her off!

A strange hooting noise made Pixie's fur stand up. He didn't like the sound of that! Nervously, he stared at the trees. There was a soft rustle, then a large bird glided silently towards him.

With a squeak, Pixie bolted. He could feel the bird gaining on him. His paws skittered across the ground as he raced back to the forest.

*Keep running — don't stop!*

The bird was directly above Pixie. In terror,

the kitten threw himself into the bushy undergrowth.

He curled up small, his heart hammering against his tiny chest. It was a long time before he dared to look up. The bird had gone but it had been a close call! Maybe he should stop searching for Princess Katie and wait until morning, when there would be less danger from night hunters.

Pixie settled down, but he was cold and lonely. He missed the cosy feeling of cuddling up with his brother and sisters. Sadly, he curled his tail round his body, sinking his nose into the fur to keep himself warm.

It took ages for sleep to come. The forest was alive with squeaks and rustles, and each one set Pixie's ears and nose nervously twitching. His stomach kept rumbling too. Pixie licked the ground, but it didn't taste very nice. He sighed. It was going to be a long night.

Princess Katie loved the palace gardens by night. The paths were lit by old-fashioned street lamps, and coloured lights shone in many of the trees and bushes. It was magical. But tonight, she was too concerned about

Pixie to enjoy it. Clutching a large torch, she hurried along with Becky, Mr Parks and Mr Parks's dog, a friendly black Labrador called Sam.

'If the kitten's out there, Sam will find him,' Mr Parks said, confidently.

Crossing her fingers, Princess Katie hoped that he was right. She hadn't realised just how cold it was tonight. Pulling her fleece tighter, she was glad the queen had made her wear it over her hoodie.

It was very quiet. The peacocks and parakeets were in their aviary, safe from foxes, and Katie felt as if she should walk on tiptoe. She kept pace with Becky, their joint torch beams lighting up the path like a floodlight. Every now and again, both girls swept their torches wide of the path, practising for when they entered the dark woods to search for Pixie.

'Don't go too far ahead!' called Mr Parks when Katie and Becky broke into a jog to keep up with Sam.

Katie wished Mr Parks would hurry up, especially when they left the formal gardens with its pretty lights behind and entered the woods. She also hoped the battery in her torch wouldn't fail. Princess Katie wasn't usually scared of the dark, but the squeaks and rustles of unseen creatures were making her stomach fizz with nerves. Catching hold of Becky's hand, she gave it a squeeze. Becky squeezed back and at once Katie felt ten times braver. But what about Pixie? How would he feel if he was alone in the dark?

*We're coming to find you*, Katie silently told him.

## Chapter 7

# A Long Night

They'd been out for ages and there was no sign of Pixie anywhere. Now Mr Parks was saying that in five minutes' time they'd have to go home!

'I don't think your kitten is here,' he said. 'He's probably tucked up in someone's home, fast asleep after a big tea,' he added kindly.

But Katie had a niggling feeling that Pixie wasn't safe. She walked more slowly, shining her torch down in the bushes, then up into trees, calling, 'Pixie!'

There was no answering cry.

Too soon, Mr Parks checked the luminous dial on his watch. 'That's it. Sorry, girls, but it's time to go back.'

He turned round, but Sam ignored his master's call to heel. Nose pressed to the ground, he followed a new scent.

Katie swung her torch wide. Through the trees, she could just make out the car park she'd been to earlier with Miss Blaze. There were lots of animals in the woods and Sam had spent a happy evening tracking them, but this scent seemed to excite him more than any of the others. Wagging his tail, Sam

left the path to nose around in the undergrowth.

Katie held her breath. What had Sam
found? When Sam gave a surprised *Wuff*,
Katie dived after him. Reaching down, she
scooped up a tiny bedraggled bundle and
hugged it close to her chest.

'Pixie,' she whispered. 'Thank goodness we found you.'

Pixie pressed his tiny body close to Katie's. His silver-grey fur was freezing cold and he was trembling with fright. Katie unzipped her fleece, popped the kitten inside, then carefully zipped it up to his chin. 'You found him!' Becky craned forward and Katie shifted so her friend could stroke the top of Pixie's head. 'Poor little thing, he looks so cold!'

'He's shivering,' Katie whispered. 'I hope he's going to be all right.'

It was a slow walk back. Pixie was so still that Katie kept stopping to check he was breathing.

'We might have to call the vet,' she worried.

'A drop of warm milk will bring him round,' said Mr Parks. 'I'll lend you a bottle in case he can't manage to drink on his own. My wife and I hand-raised three baby hedgehogs last year, so we've got all the stuff you'll need.'

Pulling out a mobile phone, Mr Parks rang his wife and also Katie's parents. Mrs Parks met them in the palace gardens with a bag full of useful things including bottles and a small animal bed, which Becky took and carried up to the palace. They entered

through the kitchens, where Katie's
mum was warming milk in a
saucepan. Even though
Katie was worried about
Pixie, she caught
Becky's eye
and managed
a smile. It
was a rare
thing to
see the
queen
cooking!
Becky
took off
her coat,
but Katie
kept

hers on, leaving Pixie tucked inside as she
continued to warm him up.

'The milk's ready,' said the queen, testing
it with her knuckle, then half-filling the
bottle Becky passed her.

'Sit down, darling,' she said, pulling out a
chair from the huge kitchen table.

Katie sat down and held Pixie in her lap.
The little kitten barely moved. *Please let him
be all right!* she thought, as she offered him
the bottle teat. Pixie was too weak to take it,

so Katie nudged his mouth open gently and slipped the teat inside.

The milk dribbled down the sides of his mouth.

'Here,' said Becky, handing Katie a piece of kitchen roll.

Katie wiped away the spilt milk and tried
again.

Pixie coughed and spluttered.

'Come on, little Pixie,' whispered Katie.
'Don't give up, please!'

'You can do it!' Becky added softly.

Weakly, Pixie stared back at the girls and
closed his eyes.

Katie nearly cried with despair. 'Please
wake up, Pixie!' she murmured.

Pixie blinked, then slowly he began to
suck. He stopped after a few sips, but Katie
was ecstatic.

'Well done, you clever little kitten!' she
said with tears in her eyes.

'He's a fighter!' said Mr Parks. 'With a bit
of care he'll pull through. If I were you, I'd
feed him every two hours tonight. That'll

get his strength up. I can take him home and do it, if it's too much for you?'

'No, thank you,' said Katie, quickly. 'I can do it, can't I, Mum? I don't have school tomorrow.'

The queen smiled. 'You won't sleep if I say no, so I suppose that's a yes.'

'Thanks, Mum.' Katie smiled back gratefully.

At first Katie couldn't bear to put Pixie down. She'd lost him once and she didn't intend to lose him a second time. She cradled him in her lap, willing him to get better. But as the kitten began to feel warmer, Katie was persuaded to leave him in the animal bed supplied by Mrs Parks, while she ran up to her room to change into her pyjamas.

Mrs Phillips, Becky's mum, had agreed

that Becky could stay the night with Katie. Mrs Philips and the queen made a camp for the girls in a room near the kitchen with beanbags and blankets. They moved Pixie's bed next to it. Katie set the alarm on her watch for midnight, the time of Pixie's next feed. Before she and Becky settled down to sleep, they nipped along the passage to the boot room together. Quietly pushing the door open, the girls peered inside. The other five kittens were crammed in their bed, fast asleep.

'They're so sweet,' said Katie softly.

'They'll have such a surprise tomorrow when they see Pixie,' Becky whispered back.

'Yes,' said Katie, crossing her fingers because Pixie was still very weak.

At first, Katie and Becky lay on their beanbags, talking quietly so they didn't disturb Pixie. Every now and then, Katie checked that the kitten was all right. His tiny body felt so fragile, his heart fluttering like bird's wings. Gradually, Katie's eyes grew too heavy to stay open. Nestling into her beanbag, she pulled the blankets up to her nose and finally fell asleep.

Katie could hardly believe it when the alarm on her watch buzzed. Surely she'd only just closed her eyes! Sleepily, she got up. Pixie was still asleep, but Becky had woken too. Stifling yawns, the girls crept along to the kitchen to fetch the fresh milk. Pixie was still sleeping when they got back, but, when Katie leaned over his bed, the kitten woke up.

Katie was about to lift him up when she noticed Becky watching her longingly. She hesitated, then bravely asked, 'Would you like to feed him?'

'Me!' Becky flushed with pleasure. 'But Pixie's your kitten . . .'

'I don't mind,' said Katie, even though she minded badly. 'You do this feed and I'll do the next one. Sit down and I'll hand him to you.'

Becky was very patient with Pixie, but he hardly drank any of the milk.

'He's still so weak,' said Katie, her face creasing with worry.

'At least he's warm now,' answered Becky as she carefully settled the kitten back down in his bed.

Katie didn't sleep a wink after that. Lightly, she rested her hand on Pixie's soft fur as she watched him sleep. Every now and then, the kitten's paws twitched as if he was having a bad dream. The minutes crept slowly by. Katie wished the time would hurry so that she could try feeding Pixie again. He had to get his strength back! At a quarter to two she switched off the alarm on her watch and got up. It was no good – she couldn't wait any longer! She woke Becky and they tiptoed to the kitchen for milk.

When Katie scooped Pixie out of his bed, he stared right at her. Smiling back at him, Katie stroked his face. The kitten watched her with solemn eyes. Then, suddenly, he licked her hand.

Katie's heart leapt. Pixie was on the mend! As if agreeing with her, Pixie latched on to

the bottle and, after a few hesitant sips, he
drank with enjoyment.

'Aww, that's
so sweet!'
sighed Becky.
The girls
shared a
smile.
When Pixie
had finished
drinking,
Princess
Katie
hugged
him to
her.

'Hello, Pixie,' she whispered. 'Welcome to
Starlight Palace, your new home.'

After two more feeds Pixie was almost back to his normal, bold self.

'Let's take him to see his brother and sisters,' said Katie, yawning sleepily. She lifted Pixie up and he snuggled into her lilac dressing gown.

Quietly, the girls walked to the boot room. Becky pushed the door open.

'Aw! They're still asleep,' she said.

Katie put Pixie down. At first, he was a bit wobbly, but, after a few seconds, he sniffed the basket full of kittens. He stepped forward silently and suddenly pounced, landing in the basket on top of everyone!

The kittens scrambled up, squeaking and meowing with surprise. Katie and Becky couldn't stop laughing.

'Look, they're play-fighting,' giggled Katie, as the ginger kitten tugged at Pixie's tail.

Becky sighed happily. 'Having kittens is going to be such fun!'

'It's going to be brilliant,' agreed Princess Katie, giving her friend a hug. 'I can't wait to see what they'll get up to next!'

# Princess Katie's Kittens

Collect all the kittens!

## Bella at the Ball

Princess Katie is busy preparing for the queen's magnificent birthday ball, but Bella is busy getting into mischief! Katie and Becky must hurry to put things right, or the whole ball will be ruined!

★ Coming soon ★

# Poppy
# and the Prince

# Suki
# in the Snow

# Tilly
# and the Tiara

# Pebbles
# and the Puppy

# Princess Katie's Kittens

# PrincessKatiesKittens.co.uk

Meet all the kittens

Puzzles and activities

How to care for kittens

Competitions

Book news and more!